T0145200

DAVID McGEE
AND THE
BIRTHDAY SURPRISE

Andie Campbell

To order additional copies of this book, contact:
Xlibris
844-714-8691
www.Xlibris.com
Orders@Xlibris.com

ISBN: Softcover   978-1-6698-0487-1
        EBook   978-1-6698-0486-4

Print information available on the last page

Rev. date: 01/27/2022

There was an old man named David McGee, who lived on Parkplace, house number three. He went to his mailbox everyday to retrieve bills and maybe an ad. Until one day he went to his box to find an envelope, no stamp, just his name.

He ripped it open expecting a letter, but it wasn't a letter at all. He pulled out his glasses from his breast pocket, and then he squinted at the letter that wasn't a letter at all. It was a set of instructions--go here, and then there.

Now David McGee, he was a smart old man, so he looked up the street....and then down, but nobody was there. Then he heard children's laughter next door. "Aha!" he exclaimed. "I bet they know who delivered this letter!"

And with that he stomped his way over. "Hey, you," he cried out. "Did you see anyone at my mailbox?"

"No," the children chorused, and David McGee was stumped. Grudgingly, he looked down at the paper in his hand.

1. Go twenty paces down the road. Turn right. Stop at the end of the block.

David McGee scowled. He didn't like this game. But what else could he do? So, twenty steps he took down the road and made the first right. Then he walked precisely one block. Now what?

2. Go into the store on your right. Turn left, to the second display. Just give them your name--they know what to do.

With a grumble and a sigh, David McGee did what the instructions said. The store on his right was a grocery store, and with a shake of his head, he turned left just as the note said. He passed a produce stand and then there he was--at the bakery. This must be it! The second display.

He stepped up to the counter and cleared his throat. "Excuse me," he said. "My name is David McGee..."

"Yes, of course. Here you go." And the baker handed him a large box.

A large box? What did he want that for? But he just shook his head and asked, "How much do I owe you?"

"Oh, no," she shook her head. "It's already paid for, but you can't open it just yet." She reached into her apron and pulled out another envelope. "Follow these directions first, before you do anything."

"But I don't want more directions; I want to go home! I don't have time for silly games!"

"Please, Mr. McGee," she insisted. "Have a little patience. You'll be at the end of your quest in no time, and I guarantee it will be worth it."

"Fine," he said with a sigh, and he took the envelope. He opened it to find:

1. Continue down the street in the same direction as before. Two blocks away you will find a little shop.

Another shop! This was getting old. He didn't want to go to a shop; he wanted to go home. But what could he do? So, he trudged out of the grocery and down the street. It was a party supply store. Hmm, was this a clue? He looked down at his paper.

2.   Go inside the store. The cashier will know what to do.

Inside he went, that David McGee and up to the register. "I'm David McGee...."

But the boy at the register cut him off. "Yes, of course, Mr. McGee. Here you go." And he handed him some balloons.

"What do I want balloons for? I've already got this stupid box. I just want to go home."

"But you've only got one stop left." He handed him another envelope. "Just do what this says, and you'll see what this has all been for. You'll be happy. I know you will. Just wait and see."

"Fine," said David McGee, and he took the note. He trudged back outside and opened it, now juggling both the balloons and the box.

1.   This is your last clue--I hope you've enjoyed your journey so far. Just walk down the street to the firestation, and be ready for a surprise.

The firestation? A surprise? David McGee didn't like the sound of that. But what could he do? So, he trudged on down the str eet, and soon the firestation came into view. He opened the door, and then suddenly he heard: "Surprise! Happy Birthday!"

He stared at his children and grandchildren who filled up the hall. In all the excitement he'd completely forgotten: it was his birthday.